THE PACKAGE

SABATO
GAETANO

THE PACKAGE

I returned on September 18th, 2024, from a lengthy, overseas, business trip that kept me out of country for three months.

The negotiations were around the clock and resulted in the merger of two media giants. I spent every moment locked in conference rooms filled with opposition lawyers, M & A bankers, accountants, and their overworked support staff.

The team's efforts resulted in a twenty-four billion dollars merger and millions in fees for the firm. I hoped that my efforts would be recognized in my yearend bonus.

Exhausted from the flight, I stepped off the plane at JFK International and made my way to passport control, and the baggage carousel. A half hour later, I stepped into an Uber and accepted the slow pace of the Long Island Expressway traffic, crawling towards the NYC skyline.

An hour later, we stopped in front of my Flatiron condo, momentarily blocking traffic. The curb lane was fully occupied with construction vans, delivery trucks and an NYPD patrol car.

Upon stepping out of the Uber, I was greeted by a familiar voice. Ted, our doorman, called out, "Mr. Mills, welcome home. I was wondering when we'd be seeing you."

Mustering a smile I replied, "Thank you Teddy."

Sensing my fatigue, "Don't worry about a thing Mr. Mills, I'll bring your bags up and leave them just inside your door."

I was glad to be home, "Please let yourself in Teddy. I'm looking forward to a hot shower and a nap."

"Understood sir, I'll make sure no one disturbs you. By the way, you have a lot of packages in storage. I'll bring them up with your luggage."

As I walked towards the elevators in the rear of the lobby, I wondered, is this worth it, I am exhausted.

The middle elevator arrived first. Stepping off was a neighbor whom I seldom spoke with, a nanny pushing a carriage, and a police officer who did not seem concerned with the reason for his visit. I stepped in, and pressed the tenth floor button of a twenty six story building. My condo is adequate, not lavishly decorated, more room than I need. At the age of 48, I was single, traveled more than I was home, and never had an overnight guest. I liked my privacy. Work was my life and only passion.

The next morning, I was up early and decided that it was best to start the day by tackling the stacks of mail sitting on the kitchen counter. Coffee brewed as the electric shades opened revealing a sundrenched day. I had three months of outdated magazines, solicitations, junk mail, and multiple donation requests for diseases I had never heard of. There were no requests for credit card or utility payments, all monthly bills were paid online through direct withdrawals.

My internal body clock was off by six hours, it was 8:30 a.m. and I was already craving lunch. Living in Milan forces you to adopt a slower pace of life, celebrating each new morning with a cappuccino and brioche. I already missed the smells and tastes of Milan and hoped to return one day on vacation.

I wheeled four matching suitcases into my bedroom and began to unpack, separating their contents into two piles: needing dry cleaning and dirty laundry. For the past ten years, my cleaning lady, Carmina, cared for me one day a week. My best efforts were subpar in her eyes. She would reprimand me if a sock were unaccounted for. The apartment was spotless, visually sterile.

It was finally time for me to sort through the pile of packages lining the entrance foyer.

All the packages were clearly labeled, except for the largest one. I quickly recalled what I had ordered in Italy, nothing required a box of this scale. There was nothing of real value, urgent, or sentimental in the boxes I opened. Most were casual purchases for my twin sibling who lived in Delaware. We briefly spoke once a year on our birthday, she never visited or married, our lives were different yet the same; our genetics bound us together.

The last package was larger than the others, and heavily wrapped in clear shipping tape. It was not your typical Amazon delivery. When I went to move it, I noticed that it was weighty, and that the address was hand- written, not a printed label. I was not sure why this package was directed to my attention.

Just then the intercom phone rang. Leaving the foyer area, I walked into the kitchen and picked up the phone on the wall, "Hello."

"Mr Mills, front desk here. You have two more small packages that arrived last night. Do you mind if I bring them up this morning?"

"Not an issue Teddy. I do not plan on leaving the apartment today. Any time this morning works."

"Understood Mr. Mills. I'm on my way and will be there in a moment." Teddy had a key.

I hung up and decided to step outside on my terrace for a few minutes of fresh air. I was looking north at the Empire State Building. I have never grown tired of looking at one of the world's most iconic structures.

After a short catnap on the patio lounge, I went back inside and cut open the tightly sealed box. Curiosity got the best of me. It was filled with used designer women' clothing and there was a note inside for a neighbor in 11G, Dee Miller. She was older, divorced, not very attractive, and walked her dog Fluffy every morning at 7:05. I avoided her whenever possible.

It was easy for the less attentive staff to make this mistake, I lived in apartment 10 G. The condition of the box was disturbingly tattered. Based on the smudged markings, it must have arrived on a rainy day. I made a mental note to drop it off later in the day, ring her bell, and leave it in front of her door. No need to chat.

It was barely 5:00 p.m. and I was feeling tired due to the jetlag, it was nighttime in Milan. No longer wishing to look at this filthy box, I decided to finally drop off my neighbor's delivery, its physical condition and contents were disturbing. What type of person wears another person's used clothing?

Upon opening my apartment door, I was met with an even larger, oversized package, blocking my path. I thought to myself, Teddy would never leave a package in the hallway. Maybe it was a neighbor with a similar delivery issue. I did not hear the doorbell or intercom ring. Building rules needed to be followed for orderly cohabitation.

I squeezed around the package and reluctantly made my way to the elevators. Upon returning, I pushed package with all my might into my apartment. It was quite heavy and impossible to grip. There was no legible name on the box, and the delivery address was similarly smudged, questionable. I did not want to make a second delivery this evening and made a note to speak with Teddy in the morning regarding the competence of his staff.

I rolled the box over and over to make certain it was for me. I did not want a repeat of the morning's effort. There were several faded letters and two numbers hand scribbled from a black felt marker, I was not convinced that the package was for me.

There was no barcode, postage scan, label of origin, or any typical identification markings. The base of the box was thirty-six inches by thirty-six inches, forty-eight tall, solid to the touch. Its edges were dented round as if it was thrown out of a moving vehicle. The same clear shipping tape tightly sealed the entire box and its contents. I needed a sharp knife to cut through the initial layer of tape. Someone did not want its contents to accidentally spill open before delivery.

The tape felt thicker than usual, methodically woven; nothing random in the strengthened wrap. When I finally cut open the top of the box, it was reinforced with an additional layer of orange mesh, covering a thick black plastic bag. I was growing tired of this exercise and guessed that it was sent from overseas in a battered shipping container.

I cut the mesh, lifted the last piece of cardboard shielding, and slit open the top of the plastic bag. I dropped the box cutter, stepping away from the package and its contents. My eyes were fixed, it was hard not to stare at what was inside.

Pressed against the foyer wall, hands trembling by my side, I looked on in disbelief. Clearly this package was not meant for me. I needed to catch my breath and gather my thoughts. I was suddenly terrified in my own home. The box was filled with one-hundred-dollar bills and euros, neatly arranged in bundles marked $10,000. Why would someone leave this package for me?

Most of my neighbors would have been thrilled; they had won the lottery. Tax free money they could spend without thought. Lavish vacations, expensive diamond jewelry, and Rolex watches were out of reach for many of them, dreams printed on silky magazine covers.

I am not like most people; this was not a gift. I was frightened and knew I never should have opened the package. It was not mine and someone dangerous would be looking for it. I have read what drug cartels do to people who know too much or steal from them. No one just misplaces millions of dollars, it had to be blood money.

I called the front desk.

"Teddy, this is Mr. Mills."

"Yes sir, how can I help you?"

"Did you or anyone drop off a large package this afternoon outside my door?"

Teddy responded, "Give me a moment. Let me check the delivery log. I don't see anything."

"Please check again," I needed to be certain.

"No sir, nothing was delivered to 10G this afternoon. Is something wrong?"

"No Teddy, thank you." I quickly hung up and began to tremble. I no longer felt safe in my apartment.

I spent my entire life sheltering from NYC's insanity. The nightly news was filled with cartel murders, random attacks by gangs, money laundering scandals, and political corruption.

This package was not meant for me! The person who left it would be looking for it. Yet I was strangely drawn to it, the money called me, its smell was intoxicating.

I carefully removed its contents and began to count. One million, three million, five million and still counting. There was ten million dollars in the package, five million in U.S. dollars and five million in Euros. Good Lord, what had I gotten into? I went into the kitchen and fixed myself a glass of bourbon to settle my nerves.

I needed to sort this out and not get killed in the process. I quickly realized that I could not speak with anyone, especially law enforcement. Innocent witnesses who speak with them often end up dead. No one could know. They would become targets, collateral damage, hunted by the owner, I felt sick and retreated into a world of solitude, haunted by shadows.

No one would ever be allowed in my apartment again. I started with my cleaning lady, Carmina. She was the only person who ever accepted me and my lifetime of phobias. I would lie to her for the first time and claim that I needed to return to Milan immediately and that the deal did not close. She was scheduled to show up tomorrow afternoon.

Carmina knew every inch of the apartment and would find the money, placing herself in mortal danger. I knew her family and could not put them at risk. Our call was brief, I told her that I would continue to pay her for one year. I had substantial savings and made good investments over my lifetime. I knew that I would never see her again.

I hurriedly stuffed the cash back into the oversized black bag and dragged it into my spare bedroom. This room was my only choice; it was in the rear of the apartment and had a door lock that used a key. The kitchen, my bedroom, the living area were not options. I did not want to look at the money and wished it did not exist.

Just then the doorbell rang. My apartment door handle has a distinctive click when touched. I remained quiet, waiting. I heard a key slide into the lock set, a click, the door opened.

"Mr. Mills, its Teddy, are you home? I have your dry cleaning."

I waited and listened, then walked out from the spare bedroom.

Teddy looked surprised, as if I was the intruder.

"My apologies Mr. Mills, I did not realize you were home. I rang the bell."

"No worries, Teddy. I'll take that. Are there any other packages for me?"

"No sir, this should be it for the day. I almost forgot, I asked the new guys about that package, and no one remembers making a delivery. You want me to take it back to the lobby and see if I can figure out who owns it?"

My heart was beating faster, as if I was running for my life. I replied, "I should have called you earlier; it was for me. No need to ever mention it again."

Teddy left, I locked the door, and exhaled, I trusted no one. I immediately went online and revoked the staffs PTE access, permission to enter. I did not know who dropped off the box and did not want to meet the person searching for it.

While on the building's website, I noticed a few changes in staffing, four in total. Their photos and profiles indicated that they were all young Hispanic males in their early thirties, union employees, contracted by the building management firm, Douglas Elliman.

I walked back into the foyer and double checked that my apartment door was locked. Using its peephole, I verified that the hallway was empty. I called a 24-hour locksmith. They showed up at 10:00 p.m. and installed a deadbolt lock, this was against the condominium rules, I did not care.

The remainder of the evening was spent going over details, the what ifs, followed by multiple bourbons, hoping to wash away this nightmare. I do not remember passing out on my living room couch.

The next day I left for work at 6:45 a.m. and planned on returning after 7:00 p.m. Work would be a needed distraction. I was afraid to leave my apartment, the building no longer felt safe. I unlocked the door, darted toward the elevators, pressed the down button, and waited. Seconds felt like hours. As the doors were closing a hand reached in blocking the sensor. I did not recognize the man.

He looked at me and said, "Hello Mr. Mills, and continued to look forward."

I timidly replied, "Do I know you?"

"I'm the new night porter, started a few days ago."

No name was offered, and I was afraid to ask.

The elevator stopped at the 8th floor, he stepped off.

Turning, he forced smile, "Mr. Mills, if you need anything, just let me know. Furniture removal, throw out boxes, bodies. I do not care what it is. I was told to take care of you."

What did he mean? Why was he in the building at this early hour and who was he seeing on the 8th floor? I returned to my apartment, I needed answers quickly. I got off on my floor and ran with my apartment key in hand. Once inside, I relocked the door, opened my knapsack, pulled out my laptop, and looked at the staff directory.

His photo was listed on the building's intranet. Carlos Fuentes, night porter, age thirty-eight. His start date was one week ago, two days before I arrived home. Nothing out of the ordinary. The 8th floor had eight units, A through H, with an identical layout as floors three through twelve. Paranoia consumed me.

I developed a twitch since opening the package and realized that I needed a plan to get rid of the box and its contents. But how? I could not bring the box to the trash room and put it in for recycling. It would be found, and the owner of the box would know that someone on the 10th floor had opened it. Everyone would be in danger.

If I tried to leave the building with the box intact, Teddy would insist, "Mr. Milo, let me take care of that for you." This would be on the CCTV that monitored the entire lobby and elevator interiors.

I immediately cut up the box into small squares and stuffed a third of them into my work knapsack. My firm had a highspeed industrial shredder in its mailroom, the tape and mesh would not be an issue. A few trips to the office and the packaging would be gone forever. No witnesses.

The next day, knapsack filled, I began my first disposal run. The elevator arrived, no other occupants, I was confident in my plan.

A few moments later, I was in the building lobby and overheard a woman near the front desk speaking with her neighbor. "Can you believe it. She sold her apartment at a steep discount; and vacated the same day.

Her friend replied, "I heard it was an all-cash deal, foreign buyer, off market. The broker from Douglas Elliman did not even know it was for sale."

"She could have gotten a lot more; everyone needs money these days."

The two women agreed that it was highly unusual and proceeded to the gym located on the lower level.

I gave it no thought until Teddy commented to me, "I'll miss her, Dee was a nice woman."

I stopped, turned, and said, "11G?"

"Correct, Ms. Miller unexpectedly sold, left all her belongings. Didn't even wait for her dry cleaning to come back."

A shudder came over me as I stepped onto the sidewalk. Suddenly, a strong hand touched my arm, "Good morning, Mr. Mills.

Hope all is well." It was Carlos, he was wheeling a luggage cart. My heart was ready to explode. I thought, I was going to die!

With more of a sneer than smile, "They moved me to days. It seems like the night shift did not need two porters. Personally, I think it was that Miller lady in 11G who complained. She was in a crazy hurry to leave the other night; even gave me her apartment keys to return to management."

Ted carefully watched the encounter, while opening and closing the lobby door.

Pulling away, "I'm sorry, but I'm late and have to get to work."

At that moment, a police car casually pulled to the curb and two officers stepped out. The senior officer briefly glanced at me, then Carlos. Our conversation was of no interest as they entered the building. Carlos did not notice their presence.

He closed with, "Don't be in such a hurry all the time, maybe a vacation to someplace warm, like Mexico." My world was collapsing on itself like a black hole. I was not well.

Teddy's eyes narrowed. He did not like Carlos' familiarity with me and the other owners.

My employer was within walking distance to where I lived. It was Friday and the office was deserted. Since Covid, most employees worked from home. I did not bother to take off my jacket and went directly to the mail room. I quickly shredded my knapsack's contents and felt a mild degree of relief. Sitting at my desk, I opened my laptop and typed in my password. The condo website link indicated that Carlos was once in the army, lived in Corona Queens, and was married with small children. Not the profile of your typical drug dealer. An unchecked mind can imagine the worst in humans.

Two weeks passed, I did not see Carlos, and nothing out of the ordinary happened. I started to think that maybe I should spend some of the money, greed dug its claws deep into me. The money was suddenly mine, I deserved it as payment for the mental anguish I suffered. Fear momentarily subsided.

But what if the bills were counterfeit? The FBI would find me and lock me away forever. I pulled out one bill from the wrapper, it looked legitimate to me, and went to a CVS cross town. One-hundred-dollar bills are not easy to spend. The clerk looked at me, ran a scanner over the bill, and glanced at me again, I was visibly uncomfortable. The scan confirmed that it was real, she handed me the bottle of Advil and $82 in change.

I returned home and entered the building lobby. Teddy was not at the door and the front desk was not staffed. They must be busy elsewhere. I stepped off the elevator on my floor, pills in hand, and took out my apartment key. I pushed it into the lock, and it no longer fit properly. I could not open my door. I bent down, put on my phone light, and looked inside the keyhole; it looked like a piece of metal was lodged in the back of the keyhole.

A closer look at the door revealed that the top lock had also been tampered with, deep scratches crossed the brass plate. I suddenly felt trapped at the end of the hallway and imagined footsteps coming my way, shuffling feet, heavy breathing.

The hallway had two L shaped wings, one at each end. The footsteps were real and grew louder as they neared. Fearing the worst, I wanted to run, but where, I was trapped at the end of a maze. Suddenly, my neighbor in unit 10 F made the turn, carrying an empty recycling trash bin. He nodded hello, apartment living etiquette.

Catching my breathe, I went back down to the front desk. Thank God Teddy was there.

He asked, "Are you ok Mr, Mills. You look upset."

"Teddy, where the hell have you been. I came home a few minutes ago and no one was manning the desk. Anyone could have walked into the building. So no, I'm not OK Teddy."

Teddy was apologetic, "Carlos didn't come to work today, didn't even call. And one of the new guys quit. I'm covering for everyone."

Trying to regain my composure, "I can't get into my apartment. Someone put something into my lock and my key will not work."

"There's an apartment renovation going on in 10A, at far end of your floor. Maybe one of their contractors accidentally went to the wrong door. It is easy to get confused, all the floors have the same layout. The carpet, wall coverings and doors are identical."

I thought about what he said, obvious to me but not to a stranger. Maybe the person who left the box could not remember what floor or apartment they left it at.

Teddy made a call and sent up the building handyman who easily removed the metal object with a dental tool and a strong magnet. The shard was part of a broken key. Someone tried to force their way into my apartment and the key snapped.

My neighbor in 10F, cracked open his door to see what all the noise was about. He was an elderly man, kept to himself, prior to his retirement, he often traveled to Switzerland on business. I apologized for the intrusion, he nodded his acceptance, and softly closed his door.

I dared not spend another dollar. Was I followed to the CVS? Did someone in the building know that I had left my apartment? Why was this happening to me? My senses were overloaded.

I decided to tell Teddy everything, make this his problem. Hand him the bag and never think of it again. I pay a monthly maintenance fee, so I do not have to deal with these things. No, I cannot get him involved. The owner of the package would kill him instead of me, or maybe both of us. He had a family. What was I thinking?

Maybe I could burn the money. I could not live with it any longer. The smoke detectors would go off, it would take weeks. The FDNY would respond, find the money, and would call the police. I would be arrested on multiple charges. Locked away only to die on Rikers Island, a prison filled with innocent gang members and murders.

I went to work the next morning, later than usual, unshaven, wearing the same suit and shirt all week. My supervisor noticed this change in personality and warned me that I needed professional help. She stared at me in disapproval and shook her head in disgust. I was not the same man and my work suffered. I was fired that afternoon.

A strange sense of relief came over me, I left and hurried home. I dared not take my typical route, I was certain that I was being followed. Finally, stepping into my building lobby, I noticed that Teddy was upset, wiping a tear with his shirt sleeve.

"Teddy. Are you ok?"

"Did you hear? Carlos is dead. Killed in a bodega on Roosevelt Ave, near Citi Field."

The blood rushed out of my head. I nearly fainted, "Oh my God, how?"

"I heard that he owed money to some very dangerous people, he couldn't pay, so they killed him. No one has heard from his family since his murder."

I was certain that his death was connected to the money. I needed to get rid of it quickly before I became the next victim.

I could not deposit the money in the bank, they no longer accepted cash deposits over ten thousand dollars. If I tried to be slick and deposited just under the posted limit more than once, the FBI would pay me a visit. I had no doubt that I would be arrested for money laundering. No one in law enforcement would believe that a bag with ten million dollars simply showed up at my apartment door. I was now certain that I was going to end up in jail because I destroyed the package, the only evidence of its delivery.

The next day I went to a local savings and loan and inquired about renting a safety deposit box. Based on their size, I would need to rent four of their largest. Just asking the bank manager about availability raised his level suspicion. I had turned into a money launderer. What if I was attacked on my way to the bank by the cartel. They would grab the duffle bag and kill me for my stupidity. No, I needed to keep the money hidden in my apartment.

A year had passed since I first opened the package, it has been six months since I left my apartment. It had become my prison. Once pristine, it was unkept, dusty, dirty laundry sat in piles. My bathrooms smelled of urine, the sinks had leaks, so I turned the water off, not wanting to let anyone into my apartment.

I thought of fleeing the country with two large suitcases full of cash. Maybe hide out in Milan under a fake name. Customs and Border Protection CBP officers would catch me and confiscate my money. I could make hundreds of trips, with smaller amounts. Too risky and impractical. Italian law prohibited me from opening a bank account without proof of funds and restricted my stay to a few months. Fleeing to Italy was not an option.

I no longer had a life worth living, sheltered in place. Afraid to leave the safety of these walls. Day after day, month after month, I continued to decay. The tipping point had passed. There was no turning back. Without a reason to live, I welcomed death.

My mind was broken long ago. One last look in the mirror; I was not the man I once was. My body was translucent, boney, that of a corpse. With all my remaining strength, I wrote a note, folded it, and left it on my pillow for the person who would find me. I closed my eyes one last time. It read, "I curse mankind and the day I stepped outside these walls." I died that evening with not so much as a cry. I was finally at peace.

No one was looking for me or cared if I lived or died. This burden was mine and mine alone.

I spent the last few years of my life hiding from a ghost who was searching for its money. I had lost my mind in the process. Fear controlled my every thought.

It took a week for the smell to foul the hallway, that brought the authorities to my door.

"Jesus, Sarge, do you smell that?"

"I sure do, whoever is in there has been dead for a while."

Teddy had retired and moved back to Greece with his family. I had never met his replacement, refusing to leave my apartment or attend any building function. I had turned into a recluse.

The building manager had a master key for the bottom lock but not for the deadbolt. They had to force open the door, damaging the frame and adjoining hallway finishes.

The two police officers were met with a wall of black trash bags, piles of dirty laundry, stained delivery boxes with partially eaten food clinging to the packaging. They covered their faces with surgical masks, digging through the trash to find me. I was on full display, sheets worn thin and grey, lying in my own excrement. There was not a single photo of me or a family member on my dresser. I died as I lived, alone.

The Sargent shook his head in disbelief "Can you believe this guy. Who the hell lives like this?"

"What about his family Sarge, anyone call them?"

"The building manager told me he had no one and hadn't left his apartment in over two years. He had a sister who killed herself a year ago, pushed him over the edge. Some sort of mental disorder."

The patrol officer called, "Hey Sarge, you have to come in here and take a look inside this bag."

The Police Sargent followed his patrol officer into the guest bedroom.

"Holy shit, look at that cash."

"You mean to tell me that this guy had all this cash and lived like this? I will never get tired of this job. No one will believe us."

"What should we do?"

Without hesitation, "Take a few bundles of euros for you and the wife and go on that vacation to Italy she is always talking about. What city was it, Milan?"

"Yeah, her brother lives there, he is a bigshot at RAI Media, they merged a few years back with another big firm, Euro something. Thanks, Sarge."

"I've been in this situation before, no one is looking for this money and it will only go to the state who will piss it away on patronage attorney fees, lining their own pockets."

"I ran his name before we got here. This guy did not show up on any watch list, not even a parking ticket. He probably saved every dollar he ever made, afraid to spend a dime. These bills are in pristine condition. Drug dealers wash their money to make them look like they were in circulation."

"No one is going to miss a few bundles. Take what you want."

"What about you?"

"I'm retiring next month." He winked, "who knows maybe I'll meet you in Milan. Now get out of here before I change my mind."

As the patrol officer stepped onto the elevator, the Sargent followed him into the hallway, closing the door behind him.

He was alone, hesitated briefly, and rang the bell of the next-door neighbor in 10F.

The door opened slowly; an old man appeared. His features were robbed of their vitality long ago, yet his blue eyes were sharp, locked onto the officer's face. He was not intimidated by the uniform.

His tone was firm, direct, "It has been a while, Sargent McMahon."

"Yes, it has Ira. Over three years."

"Why are you here at my door, that awful smell?"

The Sargent smiled, "No sir, I finally found your money."